Dear Reader,

I, Nate the Great, am a detective.
Sometimes I work on cases with
my cousin Olivia Sharp.
She's an Agent for Secrets.
What is an Agent for Secrets?
Olivia will tell you all about it.
She works hard on her cases.
She's here. She's there.
She's everywhere.
She whizzes around the streets
of San Francisco.
Follow her!
I, Nate the Great,
say that you will have
a very good time.

Yours truly,

Nate the Great

Olivia Sharp

THE PIZZA MONSTER

by Marjorie Weinman Sharmat
and Mitchell Sharmat
illustrated by Denise Brunkus

A YEARLING BOOK

Published by
Yearling
an imprint of
Random House Children's Books
a division of Random House, Inc.
New York

Visit us on the Web! www.randomhouse.com/kids

Educators and librarians, for a variety of teaching tools, visit us at www.randomhouse.com/teachers

ISBN: 0-440-42059-8 (pbk.)   ISBN: 0-385-90290-5 (lib. bdg.)

Reprinted by arrangement with Delacorte Press

Printed in the United States of America

Second Yearling Edition May 2005

10 9 8 7 6 5 4 3 2 1

To Each Other
—M.W.S. and M.S.

For Jenny
—D.B.

chapter one
Meet Olivia Sharp

Who should you
call when you're
in trouble?

Olivia Sharp. That's me.

My friends call me Olivia.

My enemies call me Liver.

I have a best friend, Taffy Plimpton. But she moved to Carmel. The next day I went out and got an owl named Hoot. She promised me she wouldn't move away.

1

Hoot and I live in a penthouse at the top of Pacific Heights with my chauffeur, Willie; my housekeeper, Mrs. Fridgeflake; and my folks.

But my folks aren't home much. This month they're in Paris.

Mrs. Fridgeflake is home all the time. But as far as I'm concerned, she might as well be in Paris. She's always busy flicking specks from glasses, fluffing up pillows, and waxing plants.

Our penthouse has twelve bedrooms.

I use two of them. One to be myself in and one to be a special agent in. What is a special agent? A very special kind of detective, and that's me!

I have three telephones.

The yellow one is for ordinary, boring calls.

The red one is for emergency calls coming in and going out.

The blue one is a direct line to my cousin Nate the Great, the world-famous detective. As you can see, being a detective runs in the family.

chapter two

How I Got Started

I wasn't always a special agent. After Taffy moved away, I used to sit around a lot in my furry white chair and look out my huge living room window at the

boats going back and forth in San
Francisco Bay.

Fantastic view.

But even when I looked at it with Hoot
on my shoulder, I still felt lonely.

I'd never tell anybody that!

It was my secret.

My problem.

One night I said to Hoot, "I bet there
must be a trillion secret problems out
there. Waiting to be solved."

I'm good at solving problems, except for
my own.

I'm good at keeping secrets, too.

I kept talking to Hoot. "If you're good at something, you shouldn't waste it, right?"

Hoot looked at me, silent but wise.

I could tell her answer was a definite YES.

chapter three

In Business

That's when I, Olivia Sharp, got into the agent business.

The next day I had Willie drive me to a printshop.

I had some ads printed up.

They all said:

DO YOU HAVE A
SECRET PROBLEM?
ARE YOU IN TROUBLE?
DO YOU NEED HELP?
YOU NEED ME.

CALL OLIVIA SHARP,
Agent for Secrets
555-4848

Willie and I put up the ads around
the city.

On telephone poles.
On street signs.

In store windows.
At the post office.

On school bulletin boards.

Everywhere!

chapter four

My First Client

After I hooked up my special red
telephone, I was ready for business.

I was setting up my files when I got my first call.

I answered immediately.

"Olivia Sharp, Agent for Secrets, here," I said.

I heard a sigh.

Then a voice said, "The world is coming to an end."

It was Duncan.
I knew him from
school.

"The world
is coming to
an end," he
said again.

"That's what you
always say." I strung three paper clips
together. Why was he bothering me?

"I saw your ad at the pizza store," he
said. "Can you help me?"

"I can't stop the world from coming to
an end," I told him. "I'm good, but not
that good."

"You don't understand," Duncan said.
"I lost my best friend. Don't tell anybody."

"I'm good at keeping secrets," I said. "Stay put. I'll be right over."

I slammed down the receiver and rang for Willie to bring the limo around.

chapter five

A Client Is a Client

I went to the closet and got my boa.

When I hit the street, Willie was waiting with the limo. "Where to, Miss Olivia?" he asked.

"To Duncan's, and hurry. It's an
emergency."

"You've got it, Boss," said Willie as we
rolled out of the courtyard and through the
big iron gates leading onto Steiner Street.

While we rode up and down the hills to
Duncan's flat, I remembered something.
Duncan didn't *have* any friends. So how
could he lose his best one? Duncan is *so*
depressing. He's always saying that the
world is coming to an end. And nobody
likes to hear that. I know I don't, but a
client is a client.

When we got to Duncan's, I told Willie to wait. I should have told him to give me a piggyback ride. Duncan lives in a flat on the fourth floor of a walk-up.

chapter six
Everything On It

I was out of breath when I knocked on
Duncan's door.

He answered it.

Duncan's hair was hanging over his eyes

as if half his face was hiding from the
world. His socks drooped over his sneakers,
and his baggy blue jeans were slipping over
his hips.

All of Duncan seemed to be on the way
down. This guy was a real downer,
all right!

"Where did you lose this best friend of yours, and who is he?" I asked Duncan.

"It's Desiree, and I lost her inside Angelo's Pizza Parlor," he said.

"That's only around the corner," I said. "How could you lose her there?"

"We went into Angelo's to get pizza. I ordered a slice for her and a slice for me. When the slices came, I handed Desiree one of them. And that's when I lost her."

"You gave Desiree a slice of pizza and she disappeared? Did she go in a puff of garlic or something?"

I laughed and fluffed my boa.

Duncan never laughs. What with the world coming to an end and all that rot.

He said, "Desiree didn't even eat her slice.

She got mad
and left the
pizza parlor.
That's how I
lost my best
friend."

Duncan
pulled
something out
of his pocket.
"I saved her
slice. Want it?"

Duncan
dangled a limp
little piece of
cold pizza right
under my nose.

I stepped backward. Then I looked down at the pizza.

"This slice is very small," I said. "Was the one you kept for yourself bigger?"

Duncan shrugged. "I didn't measure them. I ate mine and then I went home and called Desiree. But she hung up on me."

"Maybe you can get another friend. On second thought, that's not likely. I've got it. Get another pizza—a whole one—and give it to Desiree."

Duncan's face dropped. It was always doing that. "I'm out of money. I spent my last cent at Angelo's."

"Never fear, Olivia's here." I opened my purse and peeled off a ten-dollar bill. "This should cover it. Go back to Angelo's immediately and order a pizza to go. A large pizza with everything on it. Tie a huge red ribbon around the box. Take it to Desiree's house and give it to her. I'm glad I could help."

chapter seven
A Short Break

I went back downstairs to Willie and the limo. It was a lot easier walking down than climbing up.

I always feel I deserve a small reward
when I've helped someone. I had Willie
take us to the Bon Ton Chocolate Shop for
two of their super-duper ice cream sodas.

chapter eight
A Gooey Pizza Monster

When I got
home, my red phone
was ringing.

It was Duncan.

"How did it
go?" I asked.

"Disasterville,"
he said. "Desiree said
the ribbon was pretty.
While she was
untying it,
I told her
what was
inside the
box. Then
suddenly she
gave me a

weird look and shoved the box back
at me."

I had had the ice cream soda too soon.

Duncan was still talking. "The box split
open. The pizza slid out. Now I still have
no best friend and I'm smeared from
head to toe with tomato sauce, cheese,
mushrooms, and anchovies. I look like a
gooey pizza monster!"

I could almost see Duncan dripping pizza stuff. When I started in this agent business, I never expected to have a pizza monster for my first client. But I stayed cool. "I'll think of something else," I said. "You can depend upon Olivia Sharp."

"Hurry! The world is coming to an end," Duncan said, and he hung up.

chapter nine
A Wise Solution

I went to the window and looked out at the bay. A garbage barge was going by.

I knew what had gone wrong. How could I expect just one pizza, even with everything on it, to solve Duncan's problem?

I looked up Desiree's address.

I rang for Willie.

"Willie," I said, "find the name of a pizza parlor and order fifty different kinds of pizzas to be sent to Desiree. Enclose a card saying *I hope you like one of these. From your best friend, Duncan.*"

"You've got it, Boss," Willie said.

That should take care of that, I thought. It's nice to be really, really rich and able to help others.

I stuck my feet up in the air.

I painted my
toenails and
wiggled them
dry.

I fed Hoot.
Sometimes she
hoots.
Sometimes she
doesn't.
Sometimes I'm
as wise as she is.
Sometimes I'm not.

chapter ten

A Not-So-Wise Solution

I was in the bathtub when the red telephone rang.

I grabbed my robe, rushed to my office, answered my phone, and heard,

"The world has now come to an end."

It was Duncan, of course.

"Tell me about it," I said.

"Desiree just called me. She's madder

than ever. She said she doesn't want fifty
pizzas. What does she mean?"

"No problem," I said to him. "I'll look
into it."

I hung up.

I had a real problem, but I never admit that to a client. Desiree had turned down a slice of pizza, a whole pizza, and now fifty pizzas. And she was very mad. There had to be more to this than a too-small slice of pizza!

chapter eleven
Perfect with Pointy Shoes

I got dressed and rang for Willie to bring the limo around.

"To Desiree's place," I said.

When we got to Desiree's apartment

house, we couldn't find a place to park, so I told Willie to circle the block.

Five circles later, I was out of the car and heading toward Desiree's front door. She lives on the ground floor.

The fifty pizzas were blocking the way.

I picked my way through them.

I pounded on Desiree's door.

She opened it.

"I'm here about Duncan," I said, handing her my card.

I stuck my foot inside her door while I spoke. I wasn't going to take any chance she'd slam the door in my face when she heard why I was there. That's a trick we agents have.

"Come in," Desiree said without noticing that I was already partway in.

Desiree turned out to be one of those perfect scrub-a-dub-dub blondes who ties her hair back in a ponytail with a rainbow-colored ribbon. Without looking down I knew she'd be wearing shiny patent-leather, pointy-toed shoes that she could tippy-tap across the room in. I could see why Duncan liked her. Myself, I can't stand the type.

chapter twelve
Dead Cheese and Dying Mushrooms

I flung my boa on the sofa in her living room.

I said, "Duncan hired me to find his lost best friend. You. Don't you know it's wrong to get angry about a slice of pizza?"

I knew that wasn't why Desiree was mad
at Duncan. I was fishing. Secret agents
have to do that.

"The pizza was just an excuse," Desiree
said. "I don't want to be Duncan's friend.
He's so . . . so . . ."

"Depressing?" I offered. "Totally, totally
depressing?"

"Right," Desiree said. "He's no fun
at all."

"So why did you go into Angelo's Pizza
Parlor with him?"

"He came along just as I was going
inside. He said, 'Getting a piece of pizza?
Me too.' So we went in together. When our

slices came,
he handed
me one."

"And?"

"He said,
'Have a piece
of this gucky,
yucky, slimy pizza,
which has dead cheese and
dying mushrooms
on it.' That's
why I left.
Do you
blame me?"
Desiree
didn't expect
an answer.

She folded my boa neatly and went on talking.

"Later on, Duncan brought a whole pizza to my house in a box tied with a pretty red ribbon. While I was untying the ribbon, he said, 'Here's the slimiest pizza with all the guckiest, yuckiest things in the world on it. It probably died on the way over.'"

"That sounds like Duncan," I said.

"Yes," Desiree said. "He can even make Angelo's pizza look disgusting. Who needs a friend like that?"

Nobody, I thought. That was the whole trouble. Nobody.

I took a hard look at Desiree. She
was tugging at her ribbon. Her rainbow
was unraveling. Duncan can do that to
you. Unravel rainbows and all of that.

chapter thirteen

Special Delivery

Duncan, not Desiree, was my client.

I knew what I had to do.

I grabbed my boa. "I must dash off," I said.

I left.

At the front
door, the
    neighborhood
    dogs and
    cats were
    gathering
    around the
pizzas.

"Feast!" I called as I got into my limo.

"To the main library," I said to Willie.

The library has absolutely tons and tons of books. Willie whisked me there.

I checked out ten jokebooks.

"To Duncan's," I said to Willie.

When we got to Duncan's building, Willie helped me carry the ten books up to the fourth floor.

Duncan opened the door on the first knock.

We handed him the books.

"Here. Read these!" I gasped while I tried to catch my breath.

Then Willie and I took off.

chapter fourteen
Make Me Laugh

When I got home, my red telephone was ringing.

I rushed to answer it.

But I was too late. No one was there.

I flung myself on the couch in my office.

This was an exhausting

case.

The red
telephone
rang again.

Duncan
was on
the line.

"Where have
you been?" he
asked. "I've been calling and calling. Why
did you bring me these dopey jokebooks?"

"To put a smile on your face."

"A smile?" he asked.

"Yes, a smile. That nice curvy thing
under the nose that most kids have when

they think cheery thoughts. Which, by the way, you never do."

"But you're supposed to help me with Desiree."

"Duncan, darling, Desiree's mad at you because you said awful things about the pizza. You say awful things all the time about *everything*. That's why Desiree doesn't want to be your friend."

"Are you sure?"

"Positive. Listen to me, Duncan. You just said the books

I gave you are dopey. Have you even
read them?"

"No."

"See what I mean? Now I've got
something important for you to do, Duncan.
Go to your window, look out, and tell me if
you can see the world coming to an end."

"Hold on," Duncan said.

He put the receiver down.

I waited.

I tapped my fingers on my desk.

It was taking Duncan forever.

How big a job could it be?

As last he came back to the phone.

"I looked north and I looked south,"
he said, "but I didn't actually *see* the
world coming to an end. I couldn't see

east or west because there are buildings
in the way."

"Believe me," I said, "east and west are
in good shape. I checked on them. Okay?"

"Okay," Duncan said. "So the world isn't
coming to an end. But what do I do about
Desiree?"

"Think happy. Read the jokebooks I gave

you. Find a joke you really, really adore.
Then call up Desiree and tell it to her fast
before she can hang up on you. Then call
me back."

I slammed down the receiver.

chapter fifteen

Case Closed

I waited for Duncan to call back.

I read my
horoscope.

I
arranged
my credit
cards in
alphabetical
order.

I smoothed Hoot's
feathers.

The red telephone rang.

Duncan was on the line, laughing.

Laughing!

"I found five great jokes," he said.
"Desiree listened to all of them, and she
laughed."

"Super," I said.

"She says she's thinking about being my
friend."

"Now you're getting somewhere," I said. "All you have to do is keep it up. You don't need me anymore."

"You know Desiree was never my best friend," Duncan said.

"I know it."

"*You* are!" he said.

"Not yet," I said.

I put down the receiver.

I made some notes for my files.

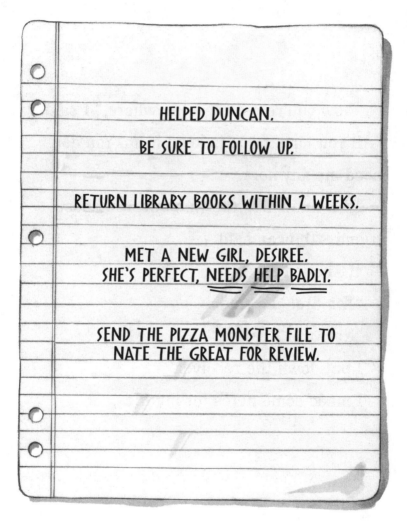

HELPED DUNCAN.

BE SURE TO FOLLOW UP.

RETURN LIBRARY BOOKS WITHIN 2 WEEKS.

MET A NEW GIRL, DESIREE.
SHE'S PERFECT, NEEDS HELP BADLY.

SEND THE PIZZA MONSTER FILE TO
NATE THE GREAT FOR REVIEW.

* * * MESSAGE TO MYSELF: * * *

SOMETIMES MONEY CAN SOLVE PROBLEMS,

BUT SOMETIMES IT CAN'T.

I closed my files and turned out the light in my office.

I went into my other bedroom to be myself.

Tomorrow I'm going to school.

Sometimes I'm a regular kid.

Sometimes I'm not.